TIMOTHY'S
TALES FROM
HILLTOP SCHOOL

ROSEMARY WELLS

VIKING

VIKING
Published by the Penguin Group
Penguin Putnam Books for Young Readers, 345 Hudson Street, New York, New York 10014, U.S.A.
Penguin Books Ltd, 80 Strand, London WC2R ORL, England
Penguin Books Australia Ltd, Ringwood, Victoria, Australia
Penguin Books Canada Ltd, 10 Alcorn Avenue, Toronto, Ontario, Canada M4V 3B2
Penguin Books (N.Z.) Ltd, 182-190 Wairau Road, Auckland 10, New Zealand

Penguin Books Ltd, Registered Offices: Harmondsworth, Middlesex, England

First published in 2002 by Viking, a division of Penguin Putnam Books for Young Readers.

1 3 5 7 9 10 8 6 4 2

Copyright © Rosemary Wells, 2002
Illustrations by Rosemary Wells with Jody Wheeler

LIBRARY OF CONGRESS CATALOGING-IN-PUBLICATION DATA
Wells, Rosemary.
Timothy's tales from Hilltop School / by Rosemary Wells ; illustrated
by Rosemary Wells with Jody Wheeler.
p. cm.
Summary: A collection of six stories featuring the teachers and students
of Hilltop School as they learn about taking turns, working together, and never giving up.
ISBN 0-670-03554-8 (hardcover)
[1. Schools—Fiction. 2. Animals—Fiction.] I. Wheeler, Jody, ill. II. Title.
PZ7.W46843 Tk 2002
[E]—dc21
2001007360

Printed in Hong Kong
Set in Minister, Cafeteria

Contents

Fritz Tries Again

ON MONDAY MORNING, Mr. Wagweed said, "It's Science Fair week, boys and girls! Saturday morning, prizes will go to the best projects."

"I'm going to win! I am going to build a rocket ship!" shouted Claude.

"I am going to grow a moss garden," said Yoko.

Timothy wanted to collect seashells.

Fritz raised his hand.

"What are you going to do, Fritz?" asked Mr. Wagweed.

Fritz drew a diagram on the blackboard.

Doris guessed it was an automatic bird feeder.

5

Charles guessed a train.

Mr. Wagweed couldn't guess at all.

"It's a Superconducting Super Collider," said Fritz.

"But Fritz," said Mr. Wagweed, "there is only one of those in the world, and it wasn't even finished. It is a fifty-four-mile tunnel shaped like a circle. It cost eleven billion dollars to build. No one knows if it would have worked."

"Well, there is going to be a second one right here at Hilltop School," said Fritz. "And this one will work."

Claude went home to build his rocket ship.

Timothy went to collect his seashells.

Yoko took off to find different mosses.

Fritz looked in the cupboard. He found a giant pack of toilet paper rolls. Upstairs in his bedroom he unrolled every one. Soon the floor and bed and chair were covered with toilet paper. But Fritz had twelve cardboard tubes.

"I need more," said Fritz to himself.

"I am going to the store. What do we need?" called Fritz's dad.

"Look in the cupboard, dear!" answered Fritz's mama.

"We are out of toilet paper," muttered Fritz's dad.

Soon Fritz's dad came back from the store with two twelve packs of toilet paper.

Fritz waited for his father to go out and start the lawn mower. Then he took both twelve packs into his room and unrolled them all.

"Now I have lots and lots of tubes," said Fritz.

Fritz decided to glue the tubes into a great big circle.

"Dinnertime!" called Fritz's mother.

"What are you making up there, son?" asked Fritz's dad.

"A Superconducting Super Collider," said Fritz.

"What's that, dear?" asked Fritz's mother.

"You shoot particles at extremely high speeds around a tunnel," said Fritz. "They go so fast that the molecules change. When they stop, they have changed into something else."

"What are they going to start out as?" asked Fritz's mother.

"Marbles," said Fritz.

"And what will they turn into?" asked Fritz's father.

"I don't know yet. Probably Bubble Pops," said Fritz.

Tuesday morning Mr. Wagweed asked how the Science Fair projects were coming along.

Doris told everybody about her cloud chart.

Nora was busy collecting bird eggshells.

Charles was arranging objects on a "How heavy is it?" scale.

Fritz was having trouble. He put his marbles into his Dragon-Slayer Slingshot, but the marbles would not shoot around the tunnel.

"Are you sure you don't want to try something else instead?" asked Mr. Wagweed.

"Tonight I will try shooting bath beads," said Fritz.

But the bath beads did not work.

"How about an easier project, son?" said Fritz's dad.

"I am going to make my Superconducting Super Collider work!" said Fritz.

Wednesday night he tried shooting chewing-gum balls.

But the chewing-gum balls didn't go any faster.

Thursday Fritz tried the pop pearls from his mama's necklace.

Nothing went fast enough to change into something else.

The toilet-roll tunnel began to sag.

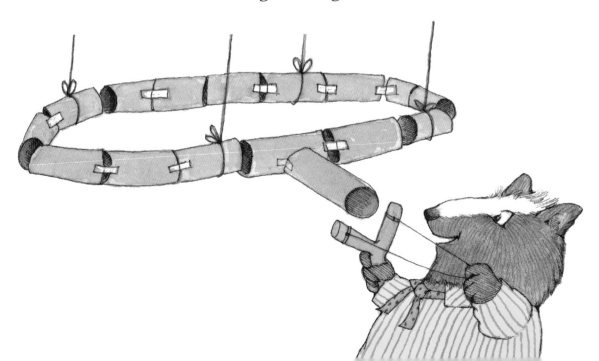

Fritz's mother shook her head. "You could imitate birdcalls on your tin whistle," she suggested.

Fritz duct-taped his tunnel and hung it from the ceiling.

"I'm going to try frozen peas," said Fritz.

"Outside, please," said Fritz's mother.

*　*　*

Friday afternoon everyone was very excited. Saturday morning was the Science Fair. Who would win the prizes?

Everyone in Mr. Wagweed's class brought in a project.

Grace's pansy seeds had begun to sprout in their see-through flowerpots.

One Frank brought in a can of motor oil. The other Frank had a jar of water. They poured both into a blender.

"See!" said the Franks. "You could shake it all day but it won't mix."

"How about you, Fritz?" asked Mr. Wagweed.

But Fritz's Superconducting Super Collider had fallen apart in the car. He tried to put it together in the classroom. He tried a bigger elastic band in the Dragon-Slayer Slingshot. Nothing worked.

Fritz did not want to cry, but he did.

Mr. Wagweed took Fritz next door into the chemistry lab.

"Now Claude will win with his rocket ship," sobbed Fritz, "and I won't have anything in the fair at all!"

"Let's look at it another way," said Mr. Wagweed. "Even the eleven-billion-dollar Superconducting Super Collider doesn't work."

"I guess not," said Fritz, blowing his nose.

"You did not give up, Fritz. You tried and tried," said Mr. Wagweed. "That is what makes a good scientist."

"Really?" asked Fritz.

"Really!" said Mr. Wagweed. "Then a good scientist tries something else. Now why don't you go home and do an experiment with an egg timer and an ice cube."

Fritz hummed the whole way home on the school bus.

But he did not want to make anything with an egg timer and an ice cube.

When no one was looking, Fritz went down to the basement. In the corner was an old popcorn popper. Fritz brought it upstairs to his room. He put in new batteries. He poured in a whole jar of popcorn.

Fritz found a sack of flour in the kitchen cupboard. Until suppertime, he shredded toilet paper into little bits and mixed them in a bucket with flour and water. He made a perfect cone around the popcorn popper and painted it green.

"That smells like boat paint," said Fritz's father.

"Oh Fritz," said Fritz's mother. "What have you got in your room?"

"You'll find out soon!" said Fritz.

The next day, Claude launched his space rocket.

"Wow!" yelled the class.

Nora had found fifty-six bird eggshells.

"Wow!" said the class.

"Look at all those seashells!" said Mr. Wagweed to Timothy.

Fritz waited for everyone else to finish. Then he wheeled in his project.

"What is it?" said Mr. Wagweed.

Fritz just smiled. Then he pushed the switch under the big green cone. The cone hummed and sputtered. Suddenly, it began to pop popcorn.

"Why, it's a popcorn volcano!" said Mr. Wagweed.

It popped corn as high as the ceiling and as far as the walls. It kept on popping while Mr. Wagweed handed out the awards.

Claude won the space medal.

Nora won the wildlife cup.

Yoko won the botany trophy.

Timothy got the oceanography prize.

And Fritz took home a big blue ribbon with "Hilltop Never-Give-Up Scientist of the Year" written in gold letters.

Buried Treasure

"NORA," SAID NORA'S MAMA, "will you put a bunch of bananas in the shopping cart?"

Nora put the bananas in the shopping cart where her baby brother, Jack, could not reach them and bite the tops off.

"Now I need soap," said Nora's mother. "Let's see what's on sale."

"Mama," said Nora, "after we finish buying groceries, can we go next door?"

"Next door?" asked Nora's mama as she put soap in the shopping basket. "What's next door?"

Nora pushed the soap away from Jack so that he would not bite the top open and spill the soap all over the grocery store.

"A little store," said Nora.

"Which little store?" asked Nora's mama.

"The little store with presents in it," said Nora.

"Do you mean Gimbel's Gift Gallery?" asked Nora's mother. "That's the most expensive store in town! Why ever would you want to go there?"

"It's Yoko's birthday," said Nora. "I want to give her a special present at her party."

"Oh dear," said Nora's mama.

"What?" asked Nora.

"We have no extra money this week," said Nora's mama.

"But everyone is buying Yoko a special present!" said Nora.

"I am sorry, my little sugar snap, but I have only enough money for groceries this week," said Nora's mama.

Nora scuffed up the vegetable aisle and down the soup aisle.

Nora helped her mama, but she did not help with a smile.

"Everyone will give Yoko something special except me."

"I will help you make Yoko a beautiful present!" said Nora's mama.

"No!" said Nora. "Never mind. You don't understand!"

Nora tossed six soup cans in the basket. *Bang! Bang! Bang!*

"Not so noisy, please, Nora!" said her mama.

"Grace and her mother are probably inside Gimbel's Gift Gallery right this minute!" said Nora.

"Nothing from Gimbel's would be as nice as something you make your own self, my little sugar snap," said Nora's mama.

"I am not your little sugar snap!" said Nora.

Up the noodle aisle and down the coffee aisle they went.

Jack's feet went *swing, swing, swing.*

Nora's mama's feet went *tip, tip, tip.*

Nora's feet went *slam, slam, slam!*

Suddenly, in the middle of a cereal shelf Nora saw it.

It was a box of Health Crunch Weeds 'n' Seeds. In the box was a free emerald ballet slipper.

"Yoko loves ballet!" whispered Nora to herself.

Nora took the box from the shelf and put it in the basket.

"Health Crunch Weeds 'n' Seeds?" said Nora's mama. "You won't eat that kind of cereal. You only like Sticky-Licky Thunderchips!"

"I will eat the whole box of Weeds 'n' Seeds," said Nora. "All by myself. I promise."

"All right," said Nora's mama. "We will buy them."

The next day at school Nora was not hungry for lunch.

"Why aren't you eating your sandwich?" asked Grace.

"Because I ate four bowls of cereal this morning," said Nora.

"Guess what!" said Grace.

"What?" asked Nora.

Grace whispered so that Mrs. Jenkins would not hear.

"I'm giving Yoko a mock diamond tiara for her birthday. My mother is going to buy it at Gimbel's!"

"My mama's going to buy Yoko a charm for her bracelet!" whispered Lily.

"I am giving her a book of violin songs!" said Timothy, "with instructions on how to play them!"

"What is your present, Nora?" asked Grace.

"Do I hear birthday talk?" asked Mrs. Jenkins.

No one said anything more about presents.

But on the school bus Grace and Lily sang, "Off to Gimbel's! Off to Gimbel's! Off to Gimbel's we will go!"

For supper Nora ate four more bowls of Health Crunch Weeds 'n' Seeds.

When she came to the bottom of the box, she found the emerald slipper.

"Oh, but the slipper is too small for Yoko!" said Nora. "I thought it would fit her! I ate all that horrible cereal and now I don't even have a good present for her!"

Jack began to cry along with Nora.

"Come upstairs," said Nora's mama. "We will string the emerald slipper on a silk ribbon and make a necklace. Then we will wrap it in gold paper and put pansies from the garden in the bow."

"I wish we could find a buried treasure in the backyard and go to Gimbel's and get Yoko a real present!" said Nora.

"This is a real present," said Nora's mama, "because it is from the heart. You ate a whole box of Weeds 'n' Seeds just to make Yoko happy."

* * *

Everybody from Hilltop School came to Yoko's birthday party.

Soon it was time to blow horns, snap snappers, and open presents.

"Open mine first!" said Timothy.

Yoko opened Timothy's package.

"A music book of Suzuki violin songs!" said Yoko. "I can't wait to play them! Thank you, Timothy!"

Yoko opened Doris's makeup kit, Claude's hopping-popping frogs, Fritz's glow-in-the-dark toothbrush, Charles's game of jacks, the Franks' frankfurter coupons, Lily's gold music charm, and finally Grace's diamond tiara.

Everyone oohed and aahed when Yoko put the tiara on her head.

"It's almost real diamonds!" said Grace. "You can't tell the difference even with a magnifying glass!"

"Thank you, Grace," said Yoko. "It's beautiful."

"Well, my mama says if I can be a princess, Yoko can be a princess, too!" said Grace.

"Are we ready for the birthday cake?" asked Yoko's mama.

"One more present!" said Charles.

"Whose?" asked Frank.

"Nora's," said Charles. "Her present is very small."

"Good things come in small boxes," said Yoko's mama.

Yoko opened the paper. Then she opened the box. Then she unwrapped the tissue paper.

Inside was the tiny green ballet slipper.

"Oh, Mama! Oh my!" said Yoko, and she ran into her room.

When Yoko came out she was holding a doll.

"My dolly lost her shoe!" said Yoko.

Sure enough, Yoko's doll had only the right-foot slipper.

"You found a left-foot slipper for my dolly!" said Yoko. "I ate forty-nine boxes of Weeds 'n' Seeds cereal just to find the left-foot slipper and I got only right-foot slippers! One after another! I can't believe this! It is the best present of all! I never have to eat those awful Weeds 'n' Seeds again!"

Yoko's mother served birthday cake and everyone sang. Then everyone wore the tiara and played with the jacks and the makeup and made the toothbrush glow in the dark.

And Yoko kept her doll safely in her lap with her two shoes on for the whole rest of the party.

Charles Stands Tall

"THIS WEEK IS BIRD WEEK, boys and girls!" said Mrs. Jenkins.

"On Friday we will have a bird show. We will make bird masks and bird nests. We will paint eggs that are just the right color for each kind of bird. We all will learn to sing the different bird calls."

"I want to be—!" said Claude, but Mrs. Jenkins called on Nora.

"I want to be a robin," said Nora.

Claude waved his hand in a big circle, but Mrs. Jenkins called on Timothy.

"I am going to be a Baltimore oriole," said Timothy.

"Charles?" asked Mrs. Jenkins.

Charles looked at his toes and smiled. He drew a picture.

"Oh my!" said Mrs. Jenkins. "It's a bald eagle, Charles!"

Claude hopped up and down with his hand in the air and said, "Mrs. Jenkins!"

"Yes, Claude?" said Mrs. Jenkins.

Claude said, "I thought of bald eagles first. I saw one in the Grand Canyon! Eagles can fly half a mile above the earth at forty miles an hour."

"Well, Claude," said Mrs. Jenkins, "Charles asked first. How about a penguin, Claude? Penguins are important birds, and no one has picked the penguin yet."

Claude did not want to be a penguin.

"No! No! No! Mrs. Jenkins," said Claude.

"Franks," said Mrs. Jenkins, "you could be a pair of turtledoves."

*　*　*

Claude sat next to Charles on the school bus.

"You should never have picked a bald eagle, Charles," said Claude.

"Why not?" asked Charles.

"Because you're too small and too shy to make the bald eagle screech!" said Claude.

"I am?" said Charles.

"Much too small," said Claude. "I'll trade you a bald eagle for a barn owl."

Charles shook his head.

"How about a pelican? Pelicans can carry ten fish in their mouths without swallowing," said Claude.

But Charles did not want to trade. He wanted to be a bald eagle.

*　*　*

"Claude does not want me to be the bald eagle," Charles told his mama that night. "He says I am too small and shy to do the bald eagle screech."

"You'll show Claude what a good eagle you can be," said Charles's dad.

Charles practiced his eagle in front of the mirror.

He pointed his hands.

He closed his eyes.

He jumped off a chair.

He screeched as loud as he could.

"We cannot hear you, Charles," said his mama and daddy.

Charles tried again and again but he could not make any sound louder than a squeak.

The next morning at school Claude had something in his pocket. It was a little red truck.

"I will trade you this truck for the bald eagle," Claude said to Charles.

But Charles would not trade.

"Claude," asked Mrs. Jenkins, "have you practiced your penguin walk?"

Claude would not do the penguin walk. He wanted to do the bald eagle screech.

On the playground Claude showed Charles a little yellow airplane. "I'll trade you this airplane *and* the truck for the bald eagle," he said.

But Charles did not want the airplane or the truck.

"Let me hear your screech!" said Claude.

Charles closed his eyes. He pointed his hands. He jumped off a dirt hill and he screeched as loud as he could.

"You don't sound like an eagle!" said Claude. "You sound like a tufted titmouse!"

The Franks laughed. Claude laughed. Doris laughed and smacked her big beaver tail on the basketball court.

Charles did not cry until he got off the school bus.

His mama was there to meet him.

"You must not worry, my little popover," said Charles's mother. "Claude is trying to bully you. But you did not give him what he wanted. You stood up to him."

Charles's dad brought home a record of birdcalls from the library. Charles practiced again.

"**YEEEEEECCCCCCH!**" went the eagle on the record.

"Yeeeeeeeccccccch!" went Charles.

* * *

On Wednesday morning Claude had something new in his pocket. It was a compass with a little tiny flashlight.

"I'll trade you the compass and the airplane and the truck for the bald eagle," said Claude.

But Charles said, "No."

"The whole class will laugh at you when you do the eagle screech," said Claude.

Charles curled his toes. But he did not trade with Claude.

That night Charles glued together sticks for the eagle's nest. It was a beautiful nest. But Charles could not screech any louder.

* * *

On Thursday morning Claude had a box with him.

He opened it in front of Charles. "What is it?" asked Charles.

"It's my mother's hat," whispered Claude. "It's made of peacock feathers. Peacocks are more beautiful than eagles. I am going to be a peacock. Unless you want to trade?"

But Charles would not trade.

That night Charles's mother hard-boiled an egg.

Charles painted it to look like a real eagle's egg.

He cut eagle feathers out of paper. He made a yellow beak out of yellow cardboard.

Charles's mama and daddy were so proud.

"You are a beautiful eagle, Charles," said Charles's mama.

"You are standing tall, just like the eagle on the silver dollar!" said Charles's father.

But that night Charles stayed awake worrying.

"They will all laugh at me," he thought. "I will never be able to go back to school again."

Charles tossed and turned in his bed.

Skreek! Skreek! went his bed springs with every worried thought.

Suddenly Charles had an idea.

In the morning Mrs. Jenkins called on Nora.

Nora made robin whistles. And she showed everyone the nest she had made with three blue marbles in it.

Next came Timothy.

Timothy hung a sleeping bag on the classroom flagpole. Then he got into it. "That is how Baltimore orioles go to bed!" said Timothy from inside the bag.

Claude wanted it to be his turn.

But Mrs. Jenkins called out, "Charles!"

Charles was nowhere to be seen.

"I think he went to the school nurse," said Yoko.

Claude began to laugh. "He wants to lie down on the not-feeling-well cot until Bird Week is over!" said Claude.

But Charles did not lie down on the not-feeling-well cot.

Charles and the school nurse pushed the not-feeling-well cot into the classroom.

Charles stood in the middle of the cot.

He showed everyone his eagle's nest and his eagle's egg.

Then he put on his eagle's hood and said, "I will make the noise of five eagles at once!"

Charles began to jump and bounce.

"**SQUEAKITY SKREEKITY SKREEK!**" went the springs of the not-feeling-well cot.

"That's as much noise as ten eagles!" said Mrs. Jenkins.

"But that's cheating!" said Claude.

"Claude," said Mrs. Jenkins. "The penguin is an important bird. Do please show the class how penguins walk!"

Tubbette

MRS. JENKINS PLAYED the Lunchtime Song on the piano.

Lunchboxes popped open all over the classroom.

Yoko took out her chopsticks and ate her sushi.

Timothy tucked into a BLT.

Grace ate her sprout and cucumber sandwich very carefully. She wiped her mouth between tiny bites, and did not allow any crumbs to fall on her desk.

Doris's spray canister of Squeeze-Cheez misfired.

"Whoops-a-daisy!" said Doris.

A dollop of bright orange Squeeze-Cheez landed directly in the middle of Grace's sandwich.

"Sorry!" said Doris.

"Oh no!" moaned Grace. "Now I can't eat it! It's spoiled!"

"You are spoiled is what!" answered Doris.

"Mrs. Jenkins!" shouted Grace. "Doris ruined my sandwich. I don't want to sit next to Doris ever again!"

"Grace," said Mrs. Jenkins. "Doris did not mean to squirt her Squeeze-Cheez at you. I will remove the Squeeze-Cheez from your sandwich with a spoon. I am sure you won't taste a thing."

"Squeez-Cheez has fat and artificial coloring in it," said Grace. "It's already soaked in."

"Well, I will eat it then," said Doris. "You are a fusspot!"

"Humph!" said Grace. "You take up too much room in this class. You are too big and fat!"

"I am not fat!" said Doris.

"You are a Tubbette!" whispered Grace.

Nora and Lily began to giggle.

Mrs. Jenkins went to the piano and played the Friendly Song. Everyone had to hold hands and sing.

We get up in the morning,
And we call our neighbors friends!
We'll all be happy till the school day ends.
We go to bed at night,
But before we go to sleep,
We count our friends, one by one, instead of counting sheep.

"Playtime!" said Mrs. Jenkins.

Whiz! Bump! Zoom! went everyone out the door.

"I'm for baseball!" said Doris.

Doris took the bat in her hands.

Timothy threw the first pitch.

Doris hit the ball to shortstop. She ran to first base.

Nora threw the ball to the first baseman, Claude.

"Out!" said Mr. Wagweed, the umpire.

"Nice hit!" said Claude, "but you would have been safe if you could run faster."

"Claude!" said Mr. Wagweed. "That's not nice."

"I'm not fat!" said Doris.

"I didn't say anything!" said Claude.

After school everyone took their regular seats in the bus.
Doris wanted to change her seat.

"That one has broken springs," she said.

"Fatty broke the springs!" said the Franks.

"Tubbette!" whispered Grace.

Gus, the bus driver, pulled over by the side of the road.
"We're staying right here in the dandelions till the teasing
stops!" said Gus. "Doris, you can sit next to me."

That night Doris could not sit up in her chair.

"What is wrong?" asked Doris's mother.

"I am big and fat," said Doris. "So I am going to get smaller. I just did twenty-five push-ups and twenty-five jumping jacks and twenty-five sit-ups."

"You are not fat!" said Doris's dad. "You are a beaver! All beavers are made the same size all the way down."

"You're just strong is all," said Doris's big brother. "You could be an Olympic team boxer!"

"Or maybe on the javelin team," chimed in Doris's middle brother.

"I bet you could win a gold medal for the Ladies' Weightlifting Olympic Team!" said Doris's littlest brother.

But after supper Doris did twenty-five more of everything.

"You are going to pull a muscle," said Doris's mother.

"I am going to be thin!" answered Doris.

The next morning Doris got on the school bus very slowly.

In the middle of Alphabet Time Doris fell asleep.

Mrs. Jenkins called in the Hilltop School nurse.

The nurse asked Doris to lie down.

She took Doris's temperature. She looked in Doris's eyes. Then she gave Doris a cup of tea and a banana.

"Now I feel better," said Doris.

Mrs. Jenkins played the Lunchtime Song.

Before lunch Doris did fifty deep knee bends.

"Soon you'll be nice and thin like me!" chirped Grace.

Mrs. Jenkins blew the Playtime whistle.

"I'm pitcher!" said Claude.

Claude picked his team. Doris was not on his team.

"She's too slow!" whispered Claude to Fritz.

But Doris overheard. She waved her baseball bat in a little circle.

"I don't want to be puny and weak!" said Doris. "I'm a beaver. This is how beavers are made. I'm in training for the ladies' Olympic team ten years from today!"

"The Olympic team?" asked Claude. "Which Olympic team?"

Claude pitched the ball. He pitched it as hard and fast as he could throw.

It was a perfect pitch, right over home plate.

Doris hit it over the roof of Hilltop School for a home run.
Everyone cheered and said, "Wow! You're strong, Doris!"
"I'm in training for the Ladies' Olympic Baseball Team!"
said Doris, and she trotted around the bases without running
one step of the way.

Timothy Takes the Cake

MRS. JENKINS HAD A RULER. She also had a clock and a measuring cup.

"Can you tell me what things we measure, boys and girls?" asked Mrs. Jenkins.

"We measure time!" answered Nora.

"Yes!" said Mrs. Jenkins. "Nora, how would you like to pick a partner for a clock project?"

Nora picked Lily. "We will count every minute of the day!" said Lily.

"What else do we measure?" asked Mrs. Jenkins.

"How tall we are!" answered Grace.

Grace picked Yoko for the "How tall are you?" project.

"And what else do we measure?" asked Mrs. Jenkins. "Timothy?"

"We measure milk in a cup," said Timothy.

"Will you be my baker, Timothy?" asked Mrs. Jenkins.

"Oh, yes," said Timothy. "I choose Claude to be my partner."

"Boys don't bake," said Claude.

"Oh, yes. Boys do bake!" said Mrs. Jenkins.

"I want to change it to a model-rocket-fuel-measuring project," said Claude.

"But if you bake muffins you can share them with the whole class, Claude," said Mrs. Jenkins. "Tomorrow will be our Measuring Day party."

At Timothy's house that afternoon, Timothy's mother brought out butter, milk, and a dozen eggs from the refrigerator.

"We can do it, Mama," said Timothy. "We are big boys."

Timothy's mother smiled. "Everything you need is in the cupboard. Call me when you want the oven turned on."

Timothy picked up the bottle of milk.

"Let me handle that!" said Claude.

"You do one egg and I'll do the other," said Timothy.

Claude separated his egg perfectly. Timothy's was scrambled.

"Let me show you how to do that," said Claude.

Timothy scooped two scoops of flour into the bowl.

"That's two and a half scoops!" said Claude. "Let me do it." Claude measured the rest of the ingredients. They mixed up the batter and spooned it into the muffin tins.

Timothy's mother put the muffins in the oven.

"I can turn the oven on," said Claude. "I bet I could even drive a car!"

"Claude," said Timothy's mother, "I am sure you could drive a car, but you have to grow older before you are allowed to touch cars or ovens."

In twenty minutes Timothy's mother took the muffins out.

"Let them cool before you put the icing on," she said.

"Let's get them out of these tins," said Claude.

But Timothy and Claude could not get the muffins out of the tins.

The muffins crumbled into little bits. Soon they had a
mountain of chocolate muffin crumbs.

"You forgot to put butter in the tins!" said Claude.

"We can't take Mrs. Jenkins a pile of crumbs for the
Measuring Day party. We will have to try again!" said
Timothy.

"We will make a layer cake this time," said Claude. "It will
have ten layers. We will use no-stick baking pans."

Claude measured the milk. He counted the eggs. He
poured out the flour.

"Can I do something?" asked Timothy.

"You can clean up the muffin tins," said Claude.

Claude mixed and mixed and whipped his layer cake batter.

Very carefully he poured it into the no-stick baking pans.

"I didn't get to do anything to help!" said Timothy.

"You can learn from me," said Claude.

Into the oven went the pans.

The cakes smelled wonderful.

But when they came out they all had deep dips and chocolate lakes in the middles.

"Something is wrong with the oven!" said Claude.

"I think you left something out of the recipe," said Timothy's mother.

"I put everything in!" said Claude. "Chocolate, sugar, eggs, milk, flour, baking powder."

Claude emptied the fallen layers onto the kitchen table.

"What could I have left out of the recipe?" said Claude.

"Me!" answered Timothy.

"You?" asked Claude.

"It's a very hot day. Look at the thermometer. Let's make car-top cookies!" said Timothy.

"What's that?" asked Claude.

"You'll see!" said Timothy. "We don't even need my mama's help."

Timothy found a cookie sheet.

Then he carefully measured chocolate chips and marshmallows and Rice Crispies.

"You measure one thing. I will measure another," said Timothy to Claude.

Timothy put four rows of cookie mix on the cookie sheet.

Then he put it on top of his dad's car in the sun.

"In no time it will be too hot to touch!" said Timothy.

In an hour Claude and Timothy went out to look.

"Beautiful!" said Timothy.

"Delicious!" said Claude.

Timothy put the cookies in a box for Mrs. Jenkins and the class.

Measuring Day ended with a big party.

"How many things did my bakers measure?" Mrs. Jenkins asked.

"We measured sugar and flour and milk," said Timothy.

"And we measured how hot the oven was set," said Claude.

"And we measured time. Baking takes time!" said Timothy.

"And we measured out the exact rows of cookies on the cookie sheet," said Claude.

"And we measured how many things we did," said Timothy. "We took turns measuring things to make the car-top cookies."

"That's a lot of measuring!" said Mrs. Jenkins.

"We measured one more thing!" said Timothy.

"What was left for you to measure?" asked Mrs. Jenkins.

"We gave all our leftover crumbs to the pigeons in the park," said Claude. "We took my dad's stopwatch and measured how fast they flew in and how fast they ate up the crumbs."

"The pigeons flew at about a hundred miles an hour and ate them all up in less than three seconds! We wrote it down," said Timothy.

"What complete bakers!" said Mrs. Jenkins.

Laughing on the Inside

"WE ARE GOING TO CELEBRATE BUG WEEK, boys and girls,"
said Mrs. Jenkins.

Mrs. Jenkins drew a picture on the blackboard with colored
chalks.

"What have I drawn?" asked Mrs. Jenkins.

Charles raised his hand. "It's a big bug!" answered Charles.

"Good, Charles," said Mrs. Jenkins.

"Now does anybody know what kind of a bug it is?"

Timothy raised his hand. "A caterpillar?" asked Timothy.

"Very good, Timothy," said Mrs. Jenkins.

"Now who knows what kind of bug the caterpillar will become?"

Yoko raised her hand. "A butterfly!" said Yoko.

"You are right, Yoko," said Mrs. Jenkins.

"What is that noise in the back of the room? Is that a bug noise?"

Someone was sniffling.

"Grace, what is the matter?" asked Mrs. Jenkins.

"I had my hand up," said Grace, "but you didn't call on me."

"Boys and girls, I think it's time for the Take Turns Song," said Mrs. Jenkins, and she sat down at the piano.

Everyone joined hands and sang.

> We go to school,
> And this is what we learn:
> Everybody gets a chance and takes a turn!
> We wait in line.
> And this is what we say:
> You go first! You go next! That's the Hilltop way!

"Now," said Mrs. Jenkins, "Grace, why don't you tell the class what kind of bug you would like to be for Bug Week?"

"A fairy princess dragonfly," said Grace.

"What a wonderful kind of bug!" said Mrs. Jenkins.

Yoko wanted to be a ladybug.

"I'll be a fire ant!" said Timothy.

"I'm a dive beetle!" said Claude.

"We are a two-part screaming scorpion!" said the Franks.

"I'm not sure a scorpion is a bug," said Mrs. Jenkins.

On the school bus Nora practiced honey-bee buzzing.

Claude did dive-beetle swoops.

And the Franks made screaming-scorpion screams.

"I'd really like to have the window seat please, Doris," said Grace.

"Why?" asked Doris.

"If I don't get the window seat, I start to get bus sick," said Grace.

"You don't have to cry," said Doris.

"You can take my window seat, Grace," said Timothy, "if you stop crying."

Grace sniffed. "Thank you, Timothy," she said. "My mama always opens the window for me when I feel carsick. Will you open the window, please, Timothy?"

Timothy opened the window.

"Not too much," said Grace.

That evening everyone in Mrs. Jenkins's class planned their bug costumes.

Nora found a pair of striped pajamas for her honey-bee outfit.

Timothy stuck two pocket flashlights into a bicycle helmet for his fire-ant eyes.

The Franks asked Big Frank to weld two oilcans together for their scorpion suit.

Grace's mama took Grace shopping. They bought a princess party crown and diaphanous dragonfly wings made of peacock feathers.

"You will be more beautiful than anyone else!" said Grace's mama. "You will be the star of the show!"

For a whole week Mrs. Jenkins's class studied bugs.

They made bug pictures. They made bugs out of clay and pipe cleaners and papier-mâché. They practiced bug noises.

Mr. Wagweed, the science teacher, told them bug stories.

"Friday will be Bug Night," said Mrs. Jenkins. "The whole town will be here at Hilltop School. We will have a bug parade. The best bug will be featured in the *Hilltop Gazette* newspaper."

"Let's be a centipede!" said Fritz to Doris. "You, me, and Charles. We'll get our picture on the front page!"

Grace began to cry.

"Why are you crying, Grace?" asked Mrs. Jenkins.

"Because it's no fair!" said Grace. "They will have a big costume and be in the newspaper. All the rest of us are only one. You can't have three against one. It's no fair."

"I think it is snacktime," said Mrs. Jenkins. "You'll feel better after something to eat."

Timothy passed around the yogurts.

Yoko was on spoon duty, and Doris gave out napkins.

"I'd like apricot yogurt please, Timothy," said Grace.

"There's none left," said Timothy.

Grace began to cry.

"I'll trade you," said Nora.

"Thank you, Nora," said Grace. "Other kinds of yogurt give me a headache."

At last Bug Night rolled around.

Behind the curtain at Hilltop School auditorium, the class got ready.

Nora buzzed. Claude dove. The Franks rattled their oilcans. Grace put on her peacock feather wings and her princess crown.

"Is everybody here?" asked Mrs. Jenkins.

"Yes!" said everyone.

"Let's give a Hilltop cheer!" said Mrs. Jenkins.

"Yay! Hilltop School!" shouted everyone.

"Kerchoo!" said Grace. "Kerchoo! Kerchoo! Kerchoo!"

Grace was allergic to the peacock feathers.

She began to cry. "Everything is ruined!" sobbed Grace.

"Grace, come and be in the centipede with us!" said Charles.

"We have to have another person to hold up the tail!"
said Fritz.

"We need you!" said Doris.

"Kerchoo!" went Grace.

Mrs. Jenkins helped Grace out of the peacock feathers
and into the tail of the centipede.

"Wow!" said the audience when the centipede appeared.

Snap! Pop! went the newspaper photographer's flashbulbs.

"We present the centipede!" said Fritz. "We have a hundred
legs!"

"We eat dandelion leaves!" said Doris.

"What's that noise?" asked someone in the front row.

"Someone's crying!" said the lady from the newspaper.

"No!" shouted Fritz. "It's laughing! Crying on the outside and laughing on the inside."

"No!" said Doris. "It's laughing on the outside and crying on the inside."

"Tee hee! Hee!" came a noise from the tail.

Grace laughed so hard she jiggled the whole centipede.

It collapsed on its side from laughing.

The next day the centipede was on the front page of the *Hilltop Gazette*.

CENTIPEDE FALLS TO GIGGLES! said the headline.

"You are the star of the show, dear!" said Grace's mama.

"Oh, no, Mama," said Grace. "We all are the stars of the show!"